James Arnott

On the Painless Extirpation of Cancerous Growths

James Arnott

On the Painless Extirpation of Cancerous Growths

Reprint of the original, first published in 1858.

1st Edition 2023 | ISBN: 978-3-37515-574-2

Salzwasser Verlag is an imprint of Outlook Verlagsgesellschaft mbH.

Verlag (Publisher): Outlook Verlag GmbH, Zeilweg 44, 60439 Frankfurt, Deutschland
Vertretungsberechtigt (Authorized to represent): E. Roepke, Zeilweg 44, 60439 Frankfurt, Deutschland
Druck (Print): Books on Demand GmbH, In de Tarpen 42, 22848 Norderstedt, Deutschland

ON THE

PAINLESS EXTIRPATION

OF

CANCEROUS GROWTHS

BY

CONGELATION AND CAUSTIC:

INCLUDING

A REPORT OF THE RECENT USE OF PROLONGED CONGELATION
IN THE CANCER WARDS OF THE MIDDLESEX HOSPITAL.

BY

JAMES ARNOTT, M.D.,

LATE SUPERINTENDENT OF THE MEDICAL ESTABLISHMENT AT ST. HELENA.

———

LONDON:

JOHN CHURCHILL, NEW BURLINGTON STREET.

———

1858.

PREFACE.

THE following pages describe a novel treatment of those cases of cancer in which it is advisable to effect a speedy removal of the growth by operation. The two measures at present employed for extirpating cancer, namely, excision by the knife, and destruction by caustic, are so dangerous, or otherwise objectionable, that many judicious practitioners have doubted whether it would not be preferable on all occasions to allow the diseased part to remain than have recourse to either. Extensive statistical inquiries have shown that, in order to obtain a very little advantage, at least a tenth part of those upon whom operations with the knife have been performed have died in consequence of them; and although the use of caustic is not quickly fatal to the same amount, it cannot be doubted that the excessive and long enduring pain to which it subjects the patient—a pain far too acute to be subdued by opium, and far too lasting to be prevented by chloroform—must, by weakening the constitutional powers, precipitate the relapse of cancer, as well as predispose to other disease.

A means of extirpating malignant growths which is unattended with pain, and productive neither of shock, inflammation, nor permanent debility, would not only be free from immediate danger, but, by relieving the patient's sufferings from the disease, and removing a perpetual source of irritation, would strengthen the constitution and thereby put it into the most favourable condition for overcoming the tendency to relapse. I have discovered that such a means exists, in the combination of long continued congelation with caustic.

Although I had been for some time aware that this expedient constitutes an infinitely better mode of extirpating cancerous growths than either excision or caustic, I was unwilling to bring it forward without the most indisputable evidence of its excellence. The past year was especially unpropitious for such an announcement. A persuasion very generally prevailed that a mode of removing cancer had been discovered in America free from the hazards and objections of former modes; and although it is now ascertained that this was only a well known caustic in disguise, the very exposure has had an unfavourable effect. It has strengthened the long existing prejudice and incredulity in regard to cures for cancer. Under these circumstances it was desirable that the strongest evidence should be adduced. With this view, permission was requested of the Governors of the Middlesex Hospital to exhibit the new remedy in the cancer wards of that institution; and the report of the cases in which congelation was employed on that occasion, forms the principal part of the present communication. These cases demonstrate the momentous surgical fact, that cancerous growths may not only be extirpated without pain, but with very little danger, either immediate or remote. Whether the new method possesses the great additional advantage of preventing relapse by destroying the vitality of the cancer germs lurking in the vicinity of the growth, as well as by preserving the constitutional powers of the patient, can only be ascertained after the lapse of many years.

The present work must be considered as an appendix to my former publication on cancer, in which those remedial measures are pointed out that will often render the removal of cancer by operation unnecessary. In that work it is admitted that some curative methods of speedier operation than those described in it may sometimes be advisable, but I was not then aware that for such cases a different mode of employing congelation from that in which it is employed for dispelling the tumour, constitutes, in combination with another agent, a plan of treatment free from every defect.

As it has been said by Dr. Simpson and Mr. Syme that the pain from caustic (often intensely severe, after each application, for many hours) can be suppressed by chloroform, it is necessary to notice an opinion supported by so high an authority. Instead, however, of entering into any fresh disquisition on the subject, I have appended to this work a recently published tract on chloroform; shewing with what risk the administration of it, even for short periods, is attended in wounds. The removal of cancer by caustic is a proceeding attended with dangers of the same kind as those which have made the administration of chloroform the cause of so great an increase of mortality after operations.*

The objection that has sometimes been made to the removal of cancer by local means, that if even the local affection could be perfectly or permanently removed by them, they would be of no service, as the disease is constitutional, is not a well founded objection. Another common disease, consumption, is also an affection of the constitution, but supposing it could be effected, would there be no advantage in removing tubercles from the lungs and healing the ulcers caused by them? General diseases prove fatal by their local manifestations or effects, and if these can be prevented or removed without injury to the constitution, the patient's safety will often be secured. To neglect local measures under these circumstances would be as absurd as to refuse to

---

* It was stated, at the last meeting of the Medical Society of London, that there is a general disuse of chloroform in the provincial hospitals of England. In the hospital at Leeds, it has never, I believe, been much employed.

extinguish a room on fire from the escape of gas because the whole house was pervaded by pipes containing the dangerous substance. There are no other but local means to have recourse to in cancer, unless it be such general measures as are adopted for strengthening the system. The maturely formed opinion of an eminent authority on cancer is, that "we are altogether unacquainted with any kind of constitutional treatment which enables us to counteract the tendency to morbid growths or check their progress when formed."[*] Under these circumstances our endeavour must be to render the local measures of treatment as safe and as efficacious as possible; nor should we forget that the doctrine of cancer being in every instance, and in all its stages, a constitutional disease, is by no means incontestable.

Another objection which has been made to this particular measure of congelation is, that it is difficult and troublesome to apply it properly. But, though this is a circumstance to be regretted, it ought not to be considered an objection. Difficulty, if surmountable, should not constitute an argument against any remedial proceeding for which there is no substitute. Few surgeons familiar with the mechanical and chemical principles involved in the process, and who will take the necessary pains, will fail in learning to apply congelation properly; and no conscien-

---

[*] Dr. Hughes Bennett, *Midland Journal of Medical Science*, January 1858.

tious surgeon will object to what is requisite for his patient's safety, or freedom from suffering, however troublesome it may be. The operations for the extraction of stone and cataract are difficult, yet who objects to them on that account? But in estimating the value of any difficult or new proceeding, we must not judge by the results alone; we must learn as well whether or not it has been properly performed. In their appreciation of intense cold as a remedy of cancer, it is to be hoped that surgeons will not forget this maxim. It has been forgotten in some published accounts of the employment of cold as an anæsthetic in operations.

50, *Baker Street,*
    January 15th, 1858.

CANCEROUS GROWTHS,

ETC.

THE Treatise on Cancer which I published seven years ago, was principally the result of the opportunity that I had of studying this disease while Physician to the Brighton Dispensary; for it was during my connexion with this Institution that I commenced the use of intense cold as a therapeutic agent; and the circumstance of its managers granting separate accommodation for cases of cancer, very much facilitated my investigations.

When the application of cold could be effectually made, and the disease was not too far advanced, its progress was arrested; the severe pain so often accompanying it was relieved; and cancerous growths were reduced in size and rendered inert masses like bullets in the flesh. The congelation was applied for short periods at intervals; and though the intention was to destroy the cancer cell constituting the essence of the disease, care was taken, by limiting the time of the application, not to injure the skin covering the tumour.*

---

* An accusation has, nevertheless, been brought against these limited applications that they have a tendency to cause ulceration of the skin. If they are inefficiently used, and so as to irritate and not depress, this may be the result; but if the application be

This practice, with great attention to the general health, and the administration of such medicinal and hygienic remedies as are best fitted to purify the blood, and give strength to the constitution, constitutes, I conceive, the best mode of treatment in the greater number of the cases of cancer. When intense cold is combined with equal pressure, its effect on tumours is much increased. It is mentioned, in a late number of the *New York Medical Journal*, that at a meeting of the Academy of Medicine of that city, Dr. Sayre brought forward a case illustrative of this increase of power. A cancerous tumour of the breast, of " enormous size, reaching from the clavicle to the lower edge of the sternum," which had resisted the application of caustic several years before, was reduced by congelation and pressure to " a small moveable tumour," and the patient was restored to perfect health.

In the practice of medicine, we must often be content with establishing facts respecting the action of remedies by the evidence of experience, without being able to explain their mode of action in a manner satisfactory to every one. We know that bark cures ague, but we cannot tell how it cures it. As opinions are still divided on the nature of cancer,

---

properly made it is the best means of preventing ulceration. In a communication with which I was lately favoured from Dr. Aldridge, of Southampton, containing an account of the successful use of congelation in two cases of cancer, it is stated, that in one of these —a case of scirrhous breast in an elderly lady, attended by himself and Dr. Joseph Bullar—the application " prevented it becoming an open ulcer, which it was threatening to do in a very few days."

the explanation which I have given of the action of congelation in its treatment will not meet with universal consent; and on this account, probably, the refrigerative treatment has not been so much in use as it would otherwise have been. It would be still more difficult to give a plausible explanation of the mode in which congelation proves curative in vascular tumours, and yet there cannot now be a doubt of the fact: I have employed it in several cases with great success.*

Cancerous growths, however, will occasionally be found of so active a nature as to render the remedial measures of slow operation, now alluded to, of little avail; and the disappearance of torpid growths under such measures is sometimes so slow as to raise a doubt whether some expedient of more speedy operation should not be substituted for them.

At a very early period of my therapeutical use of intense cold I had ascertained that the pain from the actual and potential cautery was as certainly prevented by it as the pain caused by incision; and although I had always taken care to avoid such an effect, I never doubted that congelation, continued for a very long time, would destroy the textures.

* One of these is related in Mr. Haynes Walton's *Operative Surgery of the Eye.* In a letter with which I was favoured a few weeks ago from this gentleman, he mentions that he had lately under his care the child of a nobleman "with a nævus on the side of the nose that had resisted treatment under the hands of several London surgeons. Setons had been used, and it had been tied subcutaneously, but yet the mass continued to grow. Freezing twice a week for three months has effected all that could be wished."

In the combination of these two agencies, therefore, there appeared a probable means of speedily removing cancerous growths, and the trial of it on the first favourable opportunity did not disappoint my hopes. The disorganization was rapid and painless. The important fact that congelation is a certain preventive of inflammation in parts perfectly accessible to it, was a strong additional recommendation of this use of it in cancer, inasmuch as the principal danger from the usual operations arises either from erysipelas or phlebitis.

While these researches were going on in respect to congelation, the plan of treating cancerous growths was undergoing a change on the continent. Although caustic had from time immemorial been resorted to in the treatment of cancer, it was only in a limited number of cases that it was employed by respectable surgeons. They were deterred from attempting the destruction of large growths in this way, by the extreme pain which it caused; and the value of statistics being as yet unknown in the medical art, they had not learned how frequently fatal is the excision of cancer. With one of the principal dangers of excision, however, they were well acquainted, namely, purulent absorption; and it was chiefly to avoid this, that M. Bonnet, and other surgeons at Lyons and Chartres, substituted caustic for cutting in every operation in which it is practicable. The supposition is absurd that a consciousness of incapacity to use the knife dexterously could have influenced them in this proceeding. As respects the excision of the breast, no operation is more simple; and M. Maisonneuve, of Paris, the principal advocate for the caustic treatment of cancer, is celebrated for his various operations with the knife.

The powerful and manageable caustic, chloride of zinc, was introduced into this country about twenty years ago, and has ever since been occasionally used; but it is only of late that much attention has been drawn to it, in consequence of the high pretensions of a remedy for cancer employed by Dr. Fell, an American physician, and for some time kept secret, which consists of this metallic salt mixed with an inert or valueless vegetable extract. Dr. Fell informs us that the particular way in which he uses his escharotic is " believed to be original"; if such a belief exists, it is only amongst those who are unacquainted with the recent history of cauterization.

The great objection to the treatment by caustic has been the severe and protracted pain produced by it; and this objection is applicable to the various kinds of caustic as well as the various manners of employing them. Mr. Erichsen, in his *System of Surgery*, describes the pain as " lasting not only for hours but for days: more intense than that occasioned by the knife"; and M. Velpeau, in his *Treatise on Cancer*, informs us that " the majority of patients on whom he used chloride of zinc complained so greatly that they had no hesitation in submitting to the use of the knife rather than recommence its application". It is stated in the valuable report òf the treatment of cancer by caustic, lately published by the surgeons of the Middlesex Hospital, that the plan of inserting the chloride of zinc through incisions in the slough does not cause so much suffering as other plans; but it is admitted, that, though less painful than these, it is often very painful. We are told that the destruction of the skin by nitric acid (the first part of this plan) "was in almost all the cases acutely painful," and that some patients affected with epithelial cancer were obliged, on account of the severity of the suffering, "to give up the treatment and leave the hospital unrelieved." One patient mentioned in the report, describes this dreadful pain "as if the caustic were pulling her heart out."

The concealment or denial of the excessive pain produced by escharotics appears to have been a systematic proceeding with some of those who have used them secretly. In a work on cancer by another American surgeon, who has not yet divulged his remedy, I find that he actually goes the length of condemning caustic, and, amongst other reasons, for the pain produced by it; and yet, in a report of some of the cases treated by him, which Dr. McLeod, of Glasgow, has published in the *Medical Times and Gazette* of the 11th of June last, we find one of his patients stating that so much pain was caused by the application used, that "he thought he would have died"; and another, who was under the treatment for six weeks, "that during most of this time he was put to great agony—the caustic being applied, at one time, continuously for eight days."

It is not only because acute and lasting pain is a great present evil that it constitutes so serious an objection to the treatment of cancer by escharotics, but because this intensity and duration produce long continued prostration. The opiates and other anodynes resorted to for mitigation of suffering, by disturbing the gastric and cerebral functions, seriously aggravate this mischief. The constitution is thus injured, and the chance of permanent removal of the tumour, or even of a long interval between the operation and relapse, is very much lessened. The power of resistance against the poison of cancer, or the power of casting it out by the excretory organs, would appear to be reduced. During my late attendance at the Middlesex Hospital I had an opportunity of seeing one of the cases, which, a few months before, had been under the caustic treatment at that institution. It was the thirtieth case related in the published report. This patient said, that her declining further treatment by caustic was in accordance with the opinion of her usual medical adviser, who thought that as her strength had already been much reduced by the suffering she had experienced, there would be great danger in continuing the remedy. In another case which I lately saw in private practice, and in which much pain had been endured, the patient was brought from perfect health to a state of great debility by hectic fever; and already, after an interval of less than three months, symptoms of relapse have appeared.

The principal objection to excision is, that with

probably less power of permanently removing the disease than caustic well applied, it often proves quickly fatal. Mr. Paget has inquired into the results of 235 excisions of tumours on the breast, and ascertained that there were 23 deaths; M. Lebert met with 6 deaths in 34 cases; Benedict and Mc Farlane have stated that "of 130 operations, 4 were *immediately* fatal"; and Professor Reid's tables of the practice of the Edinburgh Infirmary, shew that of 25 patients operated upon 2 died.

The supposed principal advantage of excision is, that if it does not prevent the recurrence of the disease, it at any rate prolongs life beyond the period which would be attained without an operation. Mr. Paget, who has particularly investigated this point, states, that as respects cancer of the breast, there is an average prolongation of a few months; but he does not allow this calculation to be affected by the cases that prove fatal from the operation itself, which he believes "are not less than ten per cent."* That relapse of the disease is as certain and speedy after caustic as after excision has been doubted by several, amongst whom must be included M. Velpeau. The experience of the caustic treatment at the Middlesex Hospital is unfavourable to this alleged superiority, but it were unfair to form an opinion from so small a number of cases, and the practice of an individual surgeon.

I shall now proceed to describe the method of cure which I have adopted in lieu of these pro-

---

* *Lancet,* January 1856.

ceedings, and to point out the immense advantages which it possesses over them.

If a morbid growth is kept in a congealed or frozen state for a very long period by means of a powerful frigorific mixture, it is disorganized or destroyed; and if caustic be applied at the same time, or immediately afterwards, this disorganization is quickened, increased, or completed.

The destruction of texture can be limited or controlled with the greatest accuracy, by confining the freezing mixture and the caustic to the part by a broad flat ring, or cup, made of gutta percha, fitted to its surface and firmly pressed upon or adhering to it.

There is no pain produced by this process of destruction, because the part has been previously completely benumbed by cold; no inflammation follows it, because intense cold is the most powerful preventive of inflammation which we possess; and there is a much greater chance of permanent cure, because, from the strength not being reduced by pain or narcotic drugs, the conservative powers of nature are more capable of resisting the tendency to relapse.

The following is the case in which I employed this treatment at the Middlesex Hospital. It was watched by the surgical staff and students, and seen by several eminent surgeons not connected with that institution:—

Sarah H., aged 47, and apparently in good health, had a large deep seated cancerous tumour in the centre of the right breast. The nipple was retracted,

and she occasionally felt slight darting pains. She
had been only aware of the existence of the disease
about three months before her admission into the
Laffan Ward of the Middlesex Hospital.

On the 28th of November, at noon, a circular
portion of the affected breast, $3\frac{1}{2}$ inches in diameter,
and enclosing the tumour, was congealed for two
hours by a frigorific mixture of a temperature rang-
ing from 8 to 12 below zero Fahr. This mixture,
which was frequently renewed during the process,
was confined to the part by a gutta percha cup,
having a short flexible tube, closed by a stop-cock,
issuing from its lower border. This cup was made
to adhere to the skin by heating its margin, and two
elastic bands attached to it, and surrounding the
body, gave further security against the escape of
fluids. Immediately after removing the mixture,
nitric acid was applied to the skin by means of a
dossil of lint, and afterwards, a thin layer of chloride
of zinc paste was placed upon the surface and allowed
to remain until the next day. There was no ex-
pression of pain during or after these proceedings,
but being questioned on the subject, the patient
stated that for about five minutes, while the congelation was being effected, there was a feeling of
tingling, like that produced by a mustard plaister.
The uneasiness from this was not sufficient to in-
terrupt her account of the origin and progress of the
disease, which I had requested her to give just as the
congealing process commenced. This tingling of a
few minutes duration was the only disagreeable sen-

sation experienced during the day. She took her usual dinner while the congelation continued, and slept well during the night. It is proper, however, to state, that previously to the application of the strong frigorific mixture I had taken pains to benumb the part very gradually; and, after its removal, another refrigerating mixture was applied for about eight hours over the chloride of zinc, but separated from it by a very thin membrane.

By the middle of next day a large white slough or eschar had been produced of exactly the dimensions of the lower opening of the gutta percha vessel, which had adhered firmly to the breast till midnight. In order to ascertain the extent of disorganization, the slough was cut, in the presence of the resident medical officers, to the depth of an inch, without causing the least sensation. No inflammation followed, nor did any redness appear at the margin of the slough till the third day, when its separation had probably commenced. Notwithstanding the continued action of the caustic (which was daily inserted in the manner practised by the French), the patient's health remained undisturbed until she left the hospital. The lower part of the eschar separated on the 21st December, and when I last saw her at her own residence on the 7th January, the remaining ulcer had nearly cicatrized. As her appetite had been good during the whole of this period, and she had been able to take exercise in the open air, her strength continued unreduced. There had been no occasion to have recourse again to cold for its anæsthetic effects, and the only medicine taken by her during her stay in the hospital was two laxative pills.

I have not considered it necessary to describe minutely more than the first stage of the treatment. For, as my purpose was to shew that the pain and inflammation produced by caustic can be certainly prevented, while its action is promoted, a report restricted to that part of the treatment in which the suffering has always been the most intense, and the inflammation greatest, would have been sufficient. Whether it proceeded from the deep and lasting preliminary congelation, or from her not having been rendered morbidly sensitive by the severe suffering that has usually ushered in the treatment by caustic, the patient hardly felt what could be termed pain during the whole period, except on one occasion, when a little of the chloride of zinc paste spread from an incision in the slough to the adjoining sound skin.

The only uneasiness felt, was that produced for a few minutes while congelation was taking place. I believe it is possible, by spending a considerable time in gradually lowering the temperature, to prevent even the slight tingling usually felt on such occasions, but it would be absurd to lengthen the necessary considerable period required for the process in order to attain so trifling an object. The greatest degree of smarting which congelation suddenly produced is capable of causing in the less sensitive parts of the body, has been borne by children without complaint. When, however, the surface is ulcerated and irritable there is a difficulty in this respect to be overcome. If the congelation be suddenly effected by a strong frigorific, there is no smarting from the salt coming in contact with the sore, in consequence of the instantaneous benumbing, but this advantage may be counter-balanced by the smarting produced in the deeper tissues from the suddenness of the process. I gene-rally prefer, therefore, to lower the temperature of the part, very gradually, after having interposed a thin membrane between the saline mixture and denuded surface. Mercury placed on the part and gradu-ally refrigerated, furnishes another means of effect-ing this purpose. Such circumstances may appear minute, and their relation may be deemed tedious, but the success of congelation in its more difficult applications altogether depends on attention to such minutiæ. Yet a case in one of the hospitals was published, two or three years ago, as an instance of the unsuccessful use of congelation, in which a whole hour had been expended in producing a congelation that might have been effected in thirty seconds!

The absence of all inflammation, excepting that slight degree which is necessary for the separation of the slough, is as remarkable a circumstance in the above case as the absence of pain, and in respect to immediate danger, is a circumstance of much im-portance. I have on several occasions drawn the attention of surgeons to the important fact, that in-tense cold, judiciously employed, constitutes an unfail-ing preventive of every inflammation accessible to it; but no evidence of this can be more satisfactory than a statement recently made by Dr. V. Pettigrew, and reported in the *Medical Times and Gazette,* of the 5th December, 1827. So completely is all excessive, or injurious inflammation so prevented in operation wounds, that of ninety-three operations performed by him under intense cold (ninety of which were perfectly painless), only one did not heal by the first intention when this was desired.*

That the antiphlogistic effect of congelation is a preventive of pyæmia as well as erysipelas after operations, and that it would act beneficially in this respect after extirpation of cancer by caustic, is not unlikely, though it would be difficult, with our present limited experience, to prove it. All that can be said is, that pyæmia is, doubtless, on some occasions, the result of phlebitis, which would be so prevented, and that it has never followed any operation performed under congelation.

It is a question of considerable importance as respects the removal of morbid growths by congelation and caustic, how they can be brought to act most speedily; whether a slough formed by them should be allowed to separate by the natural process before another is formed,—whether a fresh slough should be made under a previous one,—or whether the

---

* It is very possible, however, by continuing the cold too long, to reduce the vital powers beyond the degree required for union by the first intention. This happened, some time since, in two cases at Guy's Hospital, under the care of Mr. Birkett. From the congelation being continued at least four times longer than was necessary, the wound healed slowly and by granulation.

sloughs produced should be successively removed by some mechanical or chemical means, in order to give these combined measures ready access to the living parts beneath. Each of these plans may be appropriate to particular cases. The first is the most tedious, unless a very powerful and deeply operating combination of these agents be employed, when there would sometimes be a danger of the destruction of texture extending too far. The making incisions in the already formed slough for the insertion of caustic into the deeper textures, has been practised for the last fifteen years by M. Girouard, a physician at Chartres, although it is uncertain whether M. Canquoin did not precede him in the use of this method. The surgeons of the hospital of Chartres sometimes burn holes with cylinders of caustic potash and lime, into which they insert pieces of chloride of zinc paste; and more lately, caustic has been inserted deep in the flesh, either by previously puncturing the part with a knife (the practice of M. Maisonneuve), or by injecting liquid caustic through a capillary tube.* When perfected, the third plan will probably be the best. The slough formed by intense cold is soft and may be removed by curved scissors, without uneasiness. Still softer, and more easily removable, is the slough produced by alkaline caustics; and the objections hitherto made to

---

* In my "Essay on the Present State of Therapeutical Enquiry," published in 1846, a syringe with a screw piston-rod and a capillary tube, intended for this purpose, is described.

them are obviated by using the gutta percha cup in their application. They are thus prevented from spreading, and any hæmorrhage produced by them can be immediately checked by chloride of zinc, or by extreme cold alone. The contrivance of the cup will also enable us to soften or dissolve the harder sloughs formed by mineral acids or metallic salts.* I am now engaged in investigating this subject. In certain cases, more than one of these plans may be resorted to with advantage in the course of the treatment, and more than one kind of caustic. The actual cautery may also be sometimes of service.

---

* In the November number of the *Edinburgh Medical Journal*, Mr. Syme speaks of a gutta percha ring, for limiting the action of caustic acids, as a device emanating from the Royal Infirmary of Edinburgh. Considering that the principle may be usefully extended to other purposes, I think it worth while to state, that the annexed pamphlet on Chloroform, containing the suggestion of applying a mineral acid for the destruction of cancerous growths, by means of a flat ring or open cup fitted to the part, was in the hands of three of Mr. Syme's colleagues, at the Edinburgh Infirmary, in the beginning of August; and that I had described a "deep gutta percha ring," for limiting the action of frigorific mixtures, in my treatise on "Benumbing Cold," published three years ago.

Amongst other purposes served by such gutta percha vessels, may be mentioned that of applying water directly to a morbid part, by means of the "current apparatus;" and when used for the extremities, the vessel would consist of a hollow cylinder, drawn over the limb, and made to adhere to it, by heating a portion of the inner surface of both ends. In the combination of cold with pressure in the treatment of strangulated hernia, (a principle suggested by me, in the *Lancet*, for June, 1843, and lately carried into effect with great advantage, by M. Baudens), a gutta percha vessel fitting the part, and containing water and ice, or a stronger frigorific, might be connected with a tube, giving the requisite hydraulic pressure by its elevation.

One great advantage of extending the congelation beyond the limits of the growth, is our being able, thereby, to destroy the vitality of the germs of cancer (cells, nuclei, and granules), lurking in the neighbouring textures, and frequently in parts which cannot be safely invaded either by the knife or caustic; for extreme cold, as I have explained in my former work on·cancer, will destroy these parasitic organisms without permanent injury to the structures enveloping or contiguous to them. The greater chance of permanency of cure given to congelation by this property is hardly inferior in importance to its safety and freedom from pain. Had I not discontinued my attendance at the hospital before the separation of the slough in the above case, I should have strongly advised this proceeding as a security against relapse.

However lamentable the speedy return of the disease in so many instances is, after the present operative measures, if extirpation can be painlessly performed and without risk, either immediate or remote, this misfortune will, to a considerable degree, be lessened. At a late meeting of the French Academy of Medicine, M. Cloquet presented a man from whose face a cancerous growth had been excised fifteen times in twenty-two years. Many cases of speedy relapse after the caustic treatment are, no doubt, attributable to the anxiety both of the patient and surgeon to terminate a proceeding which causes so much suffering; the consequence being, that part of the growth is left behind. The substitution of a painless process will remove this motive for mischievous haste.

The union of pressure with frigorific agents facilitates the extension of the cold by arresting the circulation through the part. They may be combined in a variety of ways, such as by pressing on the part a metallic vessel of appropriate shape filled with frigorific materials; dipping a vessel containing these into mercury confined to the part by a cylindrical cup; pressing the surface which is under the action of intense cold, with a cylinder of wire-work; compressing the air in a close cup containing a refrigerating mixture, etc. These plans complicate a process already sufficiently difficult, but under certain circumstances their adoption may be indispensable.

The destruction of the skin by this method may, by some, be deemed a disadvantage, when it is compared with excision in cases in which the skin is *apparently* sound. Yet, when we reflect that the recurring disease generally first appears in the cicatrix or skin, it may be presumed that, had it been removed, the relapse might, if not prevented, have, at least, been much delayed.

Amongst the minor advantages of this method, it may be mentioned, that the perfect relief from the severe pain produced by the disease, which will be an almost certain consequence of the first prolonged congelation, is a compensation for the constraint and other annoyances inseparable from any surgical proceeding. Instead of relieving this pain, the treatment by caustic aggravates it, and, sometimes, to an intolerable degree.

In consequence of its much greater safety, this method may be employed in cases too far advanced for the use of the knife or caustic. Nevertheless, it will generally be proper under such circumstances to have recourse, at first, to the milder or non-destructive use of intense cold; and a very short trial will show whether this milder method should be persisted in. As a statement in Dr. Fell's book on cancer may be relied upon where it is *favourable* to any other plan of treatment than his own, I will refer to a case related by him, as an illustration of these remarks. It is that of a lady (Mrs. B.), who had been long afflicted with a severe cancer of the breast. After mentioning some particulars of the earlier treatment, he thus proceeds:— " The following day (August 16th, 1854), she saw Sir Benjamin Brodie, who considered the case hopeless. He ordered the tumour to be covered with a lamb's skin, and sarsaparilla to be taken internally. In the course of a few days the disease spread very rapidly, the whole breast becoming swollen and inflamed, and the general health much impaired. On the 26th August, Dr. Julius, of Richmond, applied ice and salt to the breast. This was continued at intervals of two months between each application. This treatment was pursued until June 1856, during which time the general health was much improved, and the progress of the tumour in a measure arrested. I saw her upon the 23rd, etc." He goes on to relate, that he destroyed the growth by caustic, and that he found it necessary to remove by it a portion of two ribs with the cancer adhering to them. He performed two operations. The ulcer resulting from the first did not heal till January 1857. The date of the report is April 20th, 1857. Now, who for a moment can doubt, that it would have been more for this lady's advantage to have persisted in the use of the frigorific applications under which she had improved so much; employing them, perhaps, more strongly or at shorter intervals, than to have submitted to the dreadfully painful and prostrating treatment by caustic, prolonged for such a period. Is it probable, that in a case where the ribs were affected there was any chance of completely removing the disease by caustic? About a month elapsed between the healing of the wound from the second operation and the report of the case. Is it probable, that two months would elapse before the relapse of cancer in such a case?[*]

---

[*] Where, in another part of his work, Dr. Fell speaks generally of this mode of using cold, he appears to have forgotten the above narrative. He informs his readers that, I apply "intense cold, either by means of bladders filled with a freezing mixture, or metallic balls reduced to a low temperature." This statement, though very incorrect, is instructive. Neither of these modes of application have ever been employed by me in cancer, and neither would be of service. If these were the modes in which congelation was employed, in the cases in which Dr. Fell says he has known it to be used without advantage, I am not surprised at such a result. No remedy has suffered more in reputation from the improper manner in which it has been used. Of every ten applications of intense cold in cancer, I believe that nine have

The other point which I was chiefly interested about during my attendance at the Middlesex hospital, was the question, whether congelation sufficiently prolonged might not alone be sufficient to destroy cancerous growths; and whether, if this should be the case, there might not be some advantage in using it alone over its combination with caustic. Having already ascertained, on several occasions in private practice, that congelation maintained for one hour does not disorganize even the skin covering a cancerous tumour of the breast, I was anxious to take advantage of the greater facilities which I supposed an hospital would afford for learning what further length of time was required for destroying a tumour in this manner, and what were the peculiar circumstances attending the proceeding.

The two following cases furnished very important information upon these points.

Mrs. R——, was admitted into the hospital, about the beginning of November, with cancer of the right breast. The tumour was large and adherent both to the skin and the parts underneath. The surface was

---

been imperfect, and half the number so imperfect as to be injurious. But this has been the fate of improvements in medicine of much easier adoption or performance. Vaccination fell into disrepute for a time, from the errors of vaccinators; and the excision of joints was long condemned on account of its being mismanaged. It is owing to the same cause, that the extraction of stone from the male bladder by dilatation is so slowly adopted, notwithstanding the fact proved by statistics, that nearly half of the adults submitting to lithotomy die from the operation.

much indented at the lower part, where a scab had also formed. Lancinating pain was frequent.

The common frigorific of ice and salt was applied on the 17th November, by means of the gutta percha cup, for upwards of two hours. There was the usual tingling for a few minutes at the beginning, but no annoyance afterwards. She passed a good night; and scarcely any redness surrounded the part which had been congealed until forty-eight hours had elapsed. Next day, an incision, of about an inch in length and deeper than the skin, was made over the middle of this part without causing pain; near the edge, the insensibility was not so complete. By the third day a whitish slough, of the size of half-a-crown, had formed in the centre, and the rest of the space was covered with small vesications having interstices of a dark red colour.

On the 24th November, the breast was again congealed and for about the same period, but on this occasion sal ammoniac was added to the other frigorific materials. On the succeeding day, the slough was found to have extended to the whole of the exposed surface. As considerable redness had surrounded the part previous to the second congelation, accompanied with an uneasy sensation of heat, I was glad to observe that this had been much reduced by it. In lieu of the water dressing, I desired her to use the " current apparatus " if she again felt uneasiness from heat in the part.*

---

* This apparatus consists, essentially, of a thin bladder placed

On the 29th, the slough was observed to have separated from the adjoining skin. She had taken daily walks in the garden for some time past; and felt no uneasiness in the breast. It is important to notice that since the first application of intense cold, the peculiar sharp pains proceeding from the disease had entirely ceased.

After the separation of the slough, a third application of intense cold was made on the 3rd December and continued for three hours. As the surface to which the frigorific had to be applied was ulcerated, a little more management was necessary than under other circumstances. The sore was at first covered by a membrane of gutta-percha, upon which a frigorific mixture of gradually increasing strength was placed. Care had been taken to select a very thin membrane and one perfectly water-tight. In all other respects, the circumstances and results were similar to those of the last application.

On the 11th December, as only a small shred of the slough produced by the last congelation remained, the same process was repeated but only for about an hour. As it was inconvenient on that occasion to prolong this period, and as I was disappointed in the idea which I had formed, that an hospital would, under ordinary circumstances, afford great facilities for such a lengthened application of intense cold as

---

on the morbid part, through which, by means of two long flexible tubes, a current of cold water is made to pass from a large reservoir for any required period. An allusion is made to one of its most important forms in the subjoined paper.

is requisite to destroy the texture, when this measure alone is used, I determined upon using chloride of zinc immediately after the freezing mixture. There is little doubt that a sudden application of heat to a part which has been long congealed would hasten its disorganization, but it might also give rise to reactive pain and have other objectionable consequences. Without some such auxiliary, however, it would be necessary for the surgeon to bestow as lengthened an attendance on his patient as that to which the accoucheur is accustomed, or to leave the conduct of the process in other hands.

After the caustic had been applied for some time, the patient began to complain of pain in consequence of the freezing mixture not having been renewed, and this had continued for more than an hour when I again visited her.   A fresh mixture was then placed over the caustic, with the effect of immediately relieving the pain ; and as the refrigeration was continued for five hours longer, there was no return of it.   It is difficult, in such cases, to draw a line between the merely benumbing and the disorganizing effects of congelation ; but unless the cold applied be of a degree and continuance sufficient to produce disorganization, there can be no certainty of complete freedom from pain and inflammation.

By next morning a slough had formed. I cut it to the depth of an inch without causing pain, but towards the margin the insensibility was not so deep. This slough had not separated when I ceased to visit the hospital.

Eliza C. (October 29), first observed a tumour in her right breast, in April last. It was excised in June, by Mr. Norman, of Bath, who did not employ chloroform in the operation. There is now, (20th November), a dark red flabby excrescence covered with cuticle, an inch thick, and projecting from a circular hard mass of about two inches and a half in diameter. The pain from the tumour is at times very severe. She has also been long affected with rheumatism, and, at present, both her wrists are swelled and painful.

Congelation of the tumour was produced in the manner already related, for more than four hours. There was a little tingling at first, but the part soon became perfectly benumbed. She had dinner at the usual hour, and was engaged for a considerable part of the time in reading.

Pressure was combined with cold during part of this process, by condensing the air in the cup holding the frigorific. In order that everything may be seen, this cup may be made of the upper part of a wide mouthed and stoppered glass bottle, cemented to a deep ring of gutta percha, already fitted to the breast, and through which air is injected by a double action syringe. The inequality of the surface made this mode of producing pressure preferable, notwithstanding the difficulty, when the air is compressed, of keeping the cup in close contact with the breast.

Another similar congelation was made on the 27th

November, and a shorter one on the 14th December. After the first of these, the central part of the tumour separated as a slough, leaving a space, about an inch in depth and of rather greater width ; and when the second congelation was made, the frigorific materials were prevented from acting on this cavity. The exterior surface had sloughed, but only to a small extent. When I took leave of the patient, the granulations over the whole surface were those of a healthy sore. In this, as in the preceding case, there had been no deep-seated pain, or that peculiar to the disease, since the first application of cold.

It was this circumstance, of the total cessation of pain, which induced me, when obliged by other engagements to discontinue my attendance at the hospital, to recommend that no further destruction of the textures should be made in these cases, until it was ascertained whether or not the disease had given way to the powerful congelations already employed. It is more than probable, that though a considerable portion of the tumour remained, the cancer cells and other specific organisms constituting its essential part, had been destroyed. I had learned all that I was anxious to learn, respecting congelation as a destructive agent, though this operation of it had not been completed.

The most important fact to be gathered from these two trials is, that congelation alone, when produced by the ordinary frigorifics, will not destroy the textures in cancer of the breast to a great extent, unless it be continued for many hours. Although an inconvenience as respects this particular use of the agent, the slowness of the destructive action of intense cold is a most valuable fact, as respects its employment for operations and in the treatment of inflammatory or neuralgic disease. The subject is alluded to in the twelfth page of the annexed paper.

If there be advantages in using congelation alone unassisted by caustic, the inconvenience of its action being so slow would not be an objection. It is felt chiefly by the surgeon; the patient lies on a couch perfectly at ease, during the whole proceeding.*

It is probable that a greater degree and continuance of cold, combined with uniform pressure, would prevent that inequality of destructive effect on the textures apparent in both the above instances, but particularly in the last. It would be premature, however, to speak of this circumstance as a disadvantage. For, if it should be found that the diseased is more easily destroyed than the sound part, instead of being a defect, this inequality would be a recommendation of the method. That morbid, or adventitious parts, are more easily destroyed by intense cold than normal or healthy structure, in consequence of their inferior organization, is exceedingly probable, and is perhaps illustrated by the excavation which followed the application of congelation in the last case. Caustics also appear unequal in their action

---

* Relief from pain reconciles the patient to this trifling restraint. In the case of cancer of the womb related in my other work (page 32), the most intense pain was always subdued by a congelation of five minutes duration.

to a certain, but probably less extent. What has been called the "elective" action of arsenical pastes, by Mr. Manec, and whose theory charlatans have turned to such good account in their vaunts that their secret remedies hunt out and destroy the poisonous particles in all parts of the body, may be explained on the same principle.

By this method, also, would be more certainly secured the destruction of those germs or ultimate molecules of the disease, which, as Dr. Bennett has shewn, are deposited in the textures surrounding cancerous growths, and, from being imperceptible, escape both the knife and caustic of the surgeon.

But granting that these anticipations should be realized, the removal of morbid growths by congelation alone, cannot much excel that effected by its union with caustic. The latter is not only painless, safe, and comparatively speedy, but, if due care be taken that the influence of the congelation shall be sufficiently pervading, it will often be effectual. It is to be hoped that there will be no prejudice against the latter proceeding on account of its difficulty, and because it will fail when badly executed; but, that it will be carefully studied like those other complicated operations in surgery, which, from being the only means of accomplishing their purpose, must continue to be performed.

ON THE

EXPEDIENCY OF INSTITUTING

AN

ACADEMY OF MEDICINE

IN ENGLAND;

ILLUSTRATED BY

THE PREVAILING OPINIONS AND PRACTICE

RESPECTING

The Use of Chloroform in Operations.

BY

JAMES ARNOTT, M.D.

———

LONDON:

JOHN CHURCHILL, NEW BURLINGTON STREET.

——

MDCCCLVII.

ON THE EXPEDIENCY OF INSTITUTING AN ACADEMY OF MEDICINE IN ENGLAND,

ETC.

AT present, when the question of the reform of our medical institutions is before the Legislature, it appears opportune to consider whether a beneficial addition might not be made to those that have for their object the promotion of medical science, as well as an alteration effected in those that relate to the qualifications and well being of the members of the profession.

Amongst the former, there is much need of an Academy of Medicine, similar to that in France and other countries; and, as the best proof of this, I shall bring forward an illustration of the fact, that the most pernicious medical practices may exist in England, even amongst well informed practitioners, merely because there is no opportunity of thoroughly canvassing their merits, and exposing the fallacies by which they are supported. I shall adduce a proceeding which has deprived great numbers of their lives, while the purpose for which it is used (a purpose that under no circumstances would justify such a sacrifice), can in many instances be as well accomplished, and with perfect safety, by other means.

An Academy of Medicine, instituted for the promotion of medical science, should consist of a limited and selected number of the most talented and experienced members of the profession : and amongst its offices would be the correc-

tion of prominent errors in medical practice; the encouragement of investigation by prizes and other means; the rendering of assistance to practical inquirers, by gaining access for them to the records of cases in the public hospitals; the reception of, and reporting upon, proposals of improvements in the treatment of disease, and, when these improvements are verified, the introduction of them into practice, and particularly into the practice of hospitals. Its duties as the counsellor of Government on subjects relating to the health of the community would be of no less importance; but, being of a different aspect, need not at present engage our attention.

Of English medical improvements or inventions, it is probable that the greater part sink into oblivion, or die with their authors, because there is no opportunity of making them known and appreciated. If they are published in monographs or journals, they are lost amidst the mass of useless projects constantly issuing from the press; and if their authors bring them before the existing medical societies, they experience no better fate. We are told in the life of Jenner, that, in consequence of his persevering endeavours in some medical societies to obtain a due appreciation of vaccination, he was threatened with expulsion from them, as an "insufferable bore". These associations, though on other accounts exceedingly useful, hardly aim at, and certainly do not fulfil, the purposes of such an academy as has been contemplated. Few of those whose talents and experience would give weight to their opinions, though they very properly countenance and support such institutions, take any part in their proceedings.

Had such an academy as is now proposed existed in Britain, many inventions would not have been lost, and many, which have survived neglect, would have sooner been brought into use. The excision of joints in lieu of amputation, for example, and the compression of aneurismal arteries in lieu of their closure by a ligature, would not have required half a century to become established operations in surgery.

Many other important points in therapeutics remain involved in some degree of doubt, principally because the statistics are not accessible by which they can be best determined. Amongst practical improvements, I may be excused for mentioning one of great value, which, from want of that aid which an academy would have afforded, has, as respects its principal uses, remained almost unknown. Had there been such an institution in this country, the plan only now introduced into Germany by Langenbeck, of accurately regulating the temperature of amputation and other severe wounds, and excluding the air from them, whereby the mortality from operations and compound fractures has in his practice been much reduced, would, from the urgent necessity of such an expedient, have doubtless been in use ten years ago ; for a longer period than this has elapsed since the " water muff" for encircling diseased or injured joints and limbs, with its gutta percha " supporter" and long caoutchouc tubes to effect a continuous current, was described in my essay *On the Present State of Therapeutical Inquiry.**

But of practical questions at present before the profession, and requiring for their decision the investigation and authority of an academy, there is none of more importance than that respecting the use of chloroform in operations ; and to its consideration the remaining part of this paper will be given. One example of such questions, fully stated, will be enough to show the necessity of such an institution.

More than a hundred years have elapsed since a minute account was given, in the *Philosophical Transactions,* of the insensibility caused in dogs by immersing them in the me-

---

* That this apparatus is not wholly unknown here, is mainly to be ascribed to the accident of its being profitable to the manufacturer. Every surgeon must have seen the representation of a patient, to whom what I have termed the " intermitting current apparatus" is being applied, with which one of its makers (the first in whose hands I placed it) has illustrated his advertisement in all the English medical journals for the last six years. The most complete account of the current apparatus and its various uses is given in a treatise *On Indigestion,* 1847. It is briefly described in Dr. Watson's *Lectures on the Practice of Physic,* 3rd edit., vol. i, page 388.

phitic vapour of the Grotto del Cane, near Naples. Dr. Hickman recommended the inhalation of this vapour, in order to render operations painless, about seventy years afterwards, but not until Sir H. Davy had suggested nitrous oxide gas for the same purpose. The fear, however, of injurious consequences, appears to have long prevented surgeons from endeavouring to revive by such inhalations the ancient practice (alluded to by Shakespeare and Bocaccio) of preventing pain in operations; and it was not until ten years ago that they were actually brought into use by an adventurous American dentist, Mr. Horace Wells. A number of inhalable substances, of similar properties, have since been employed; but the vapour which has been principally resorted to in this country is that of chloroform. Although several instances of sudden death occurred from these agents soon after their introduction, it was supposed that this fatality might arise from the faulty mode of administering them; and the dread of more remote evils was completely dispelled by the publication of statistics professing to prove that it had no foundation. After no great length of time, recourse was unhesitatingly had to chloroform on every trifling occasion, notwithstanding that sudden deaths continued to occur. Familiarity with danger put an end to the apprehension of it. We had in the indiscriminate and fearless use of the new drug an instance of what Celsus calls " audacia usu ipso confirmata". Large doses were recommended in preference to the small ones originally used; and extreme debility or disease of the heart, instead of being deemed objections to the administration of chloroform, were at length spoken of as conditions in which it might be given with peculiar advantage!

Never has there existed in the practice of medicine a more pernicious error than this common and indiscriminate use of chloroform. Its advantage in preventing pain is palpable and immediate; its disadvantage or danger is, in most instances, latent and remote, and hence, until lately, it has been undiscovered. It certainly is not unaccompanied with the perils which caused the expulsion from surgery of the operation narcotics of former times.

The deaths caused by chloroform may be divided, first, into those which take place during its administration; secondly, those occurring some hours afterwards, but which, as is evident from the symptoms, are certainly the consequences of chloroform; and thirdly, those that happen long after its exhibition, and as the result probably of its having predisposed to pyæmia and other morbid affections, well known as proving fatal after the severer operations. These last, which are by far the most numerous, can only be discovered to be the consequences of chloroform with any certainty, by instituting comparisons between the amount of mortality in similar cases before and after the time of its introduction.

About a hundred instances of *sudden* death from this new practice have been reported; but there cannot be a doubt that the greater number have been concealed. Amongst other proofs of this, it may be mentioned that six times more deaths have been published as happening in the hospitals of London, than in its private practice; and scarcely half a dozen such accidents have become generally known in France. This evident concealment, of which every medical man must know instances, is not extraordinary; nor can it now be deemed more reprehensible than the concealment of fatal accidents from other drugs. For what family is there that would not shrink from the horrors of a coroner's inquest, where, as happens in these cases, there can be no suspicion of foul play ?*

---

* Although few cases of sudden death from chloroform have been published in France, and although its ulterior effects have scarcely been adverted to by continental practitioners, we find one of the leading surgeons in Paris—M. Ricord—speaking of it in the following terms, in the interesting debate on the subject now proceeding at the Academy of Medicine :—" I refrain as much as possible from the use of etherization. Etherization, in my view, is a hazard which complicates operations. It is doubtless a great discovery, and has rendered much service; but it must not be concealed that it is also a great danger. Accordingly, I never have recourse to it but under extreme necessity, or when I am strongly importuned; and, in minor operations, I refuse to employ it." (*Gazette des Hôpitaux*, July 9th.)

I am inclined to think, however, that sudden deaths from chloroform have not been so frequent in France as in England. More attention is there paid

The second class consists of those deaths, from the direct effects of chloroform, which have been attributed to other causes. Of these, Mr. Mouat, who had charge of the field hospital at the Redan, has given us examples in the cases of soldiers who never rallied after its administration, but sank "from exhaustion in from twelve to twenty-four hours";[*] and M. Chassaignac, of the Hôpital Laborisière in Paris, has recently described similar occurrences.[†] Indeed, whoever reads attentively the circumstantial hospital reports of amputations, etc., in the *Medical Times and Gazette*, during the last four years, will meet with many deaths which are unquestionably of this description.

The more remote effects of chloroform, though they may be guessed at by analogy, can only be satisfactorily ascertained by statistics. Dr. Simpson endeavoured, by returns from various hospitals, to make it appear that these effects are beneficial; and that chloroform, though proving immediately fatal in some instances, lessens the general mortality from operations by promoting, on other occasions, the healing of the wound. We must not, he argued, prohibit bathing because a few persons are drowned, for many more lives are saved by its salutary effects than are lost by such accidents. But the truth is, there can be no comparison between the exhibition of chloroform and ordinary bathing. Instead of compensation, there is much additional destruction. The administration of chloroform resembles, in this respect, bathing in a dangerous river, and the long continued stay of an invalid in very cold water. Nor can any comparison be made, in this respect, between chloroform and other powerful drugs. These very rarely prove fatal in the hands of skilful practitioners; and when they do so, it has not been for so comparatively small a purpose as the prevention of short pain that they have been administered. The tables which Dr. Simpson published in proof of the opinion

---

to the circumstances which prohibit its use in particular cases; and the employment of "inhalers" in its administration has been generally condemned.

[*] *Medical Times and Gazette*, August 31, 1856.

[†] *Lancet*, February 23, 1857.

of ultimate advantage from chloroform, and which have unfortunately been as authoritative with many surgeons as the Northampton Life Tables are with assurance companies, involve the greatest fallacies. I have elsewhere shown, that when the data on which they were founded (and which are, no doubt, authentic and accurate) are properly used, the very reverse of his proposition is proved by them.

I have renewed the investigation of this subject by statistics, and have discovered that the destruction of life by chloroform has been very great. Besides the data which Dr. Simpson had collected, a subsequent series of accurate returns of amputation and lithotomy cases from the London and provincial hospitals, have been made use of; and from these collectively, the clearest evidence is afforded that the mortality since the introduction of chloroform has increased more than 10 per cent. after amputation, and more than 20 per cent. after lithotomy on the adult. In other words, instead of one patient dying in four or five after amputation as formerly, one now dies in three; and instead of one adult dying in four after lithotomy (which is rather more than the former ratio), one now dies in two. These facts may be better understood from the following tables, which are abridgments of several published in the *Medical Times and Gazette*, Oct. 25 and April 25, and, partially, in *Ranking's Retrospect* for the last year. The authorities for the data are there given, and the principles on which the tables were constructed are explained, both in the observations accompanying them and in several controversial letters on the subject which have subsequently appeared in the same journal.

Attempts have been made to account for the great increase of mortality after the severer operations, by assigning other causes than chloroform; but while this has all the evidence of the real cause, the others, such as a decay of surgical skill, an epidemic pyæmia, the cholera, etc., have not the slightest plausible foundation. Hospitals are better ventilated than they used to be; pyæmia, though better known and more frequently detected than formerly, has not in-

TABLE I.

Shewing the recent increase of Mortality after Amputation of the Thigh, Leg, and Arm, in Four London and Fourteen Provincial Hospitals.

Hospitals.	Authorities.	Period of Observation.	Before Chloroform.		Authorities.	Period of Observation.	After Chloroform.		Increase of mortality since the introduction of Chloroform.
			Cases.	Deaths.			Cases.	Deaths.	
St. Bartholomew's	Mr. Haig.	1846	22	4	Med.Times&Gaz.	1855—56	31	9	10·9 per cent.
University College	Mr. Potter.	1835—46	103	24	,, ,,	1855—56	21	7	10 per cent.
St. Thomas's	Mr. South.	1842—47	49	13	,, ,,	1855—56	23	9	12 per cent.
Guy's	Hospl. reports.	1843—46	68	18	,, ,,	1854—56	85	27	5·7 per cent.
Oxford	Mr. Hussey.	1838—47	60	5	Mr. Hussey.	1848—56	76	18	Average increase of mortality (equal periods being taken) 12·5 per cent.
Liverpool Royal	Mr. Halton.	1835—36	43	3	Med.Times&Gaz.	1855—56	16	3	
Gloucester	Mr. Charleton.	1842—44	32	7	,, ,,	1855—56	13	6	
Glasgow	Dr. M'Ghie.	1840—46	137	54	Dr. M'Ghie.	1853	38	13	
Ten other provincial hospitals	Dr. Simpson's statistical table.	....	100	21	Med.Times&Gaz.	1855—56	112	36	

TABLE II.

Shewing the recent increase of Mortality from Lithotomy in the Adult.

	Per Cent.
Former rate of mortality, calculated from 775 cases of various operators (see Mr. Coulson's work on Lithotomy) ..	22¼
Rate of mortality since the introduction of chloroform, calculated from 81 cases in London and Provincial Hospitals (see *Medical Times and Gazette*)	48

creased independently of chloroform; and surgery, with this solitary exception, has advanced. On the other hand, chloroform has proved itself a virulent poison by the numerous sudden deaths that have happened during its administration, and by the suffocations, faintings, etc., bordering on death that have still more frequently been produced by it. That its agency is not of that transient character which has been represented, is evident from the extreme and long continued prostration that so often follows it, as well as from the persisting vomiting, headache, shivering, and other symptoms, denoting severe constitutional disturbance. But the fact that, in many cases, death has happened hours or days after its administration, and without any intermission of the unfavourable symptoms produced by it, sets this question at rest. " It would seem," to use the words of M. Chassaignac, " that the injury done in these cases to the vital forces by the chloroform has been so profound that the patient could not recover from it." Besides, it is well known that a fatal influence is often excited by causes that produce no discernible symptoms. Hæmorrhage, foul air, and intoxication, are of this description. Like chloroform, the two last are secret poisoners; for one who is suddenly cut off by these (as in drinking for a wager, or as when, on a late occasion, the passengers of an Irish steamboat were, during a storm, crowded under hatches), thousands die from the predisposition to fatal disease which is caused by their debilitating effects. Would a surgeon have no fear of excessive alcoholic intoxication interfering with the healing of the wound in a patient undergoing amputation of the leg?

Now, when we reflect that agents so powerful and dangerous as the intoxicating vapours have been universally employed in every important operation for the last six years, we cannot be surprised to find that operations so severe as themselves to place the patient in danger, should during that period have proved much less successful than formerly. On the contrary, a different result would be the strangest anomaly; and there is, perhaps, no other instance in medicine where the influence of authority and example, the bold denials of mischief by interested parties, the hopes and fears of both practitioners and patients, and other misleading influences, have so prevailed against a truth which, to the unprejudiced, must appear so palpable.. The obstinate resistance of the " hot and sweating regimen" in fevers, against the facts and arguments of Sydenham, was not nearly so extraordinary. It would not be more extraordinary if the pain caused by disease, like that from operations, had on all occasions, and with utter disregard to the patient's life, been repressed by opium. Narcotism or stupefaction, whether produced by chloroform or Godfrey's cordial, is a certain preventive of pain however originating ; but it is surely an important question on what occasions it ought to be had recourse to, and whether the patient's safety ought always to be sacrificed to his ease.

It is necessary, however, to advert to a great misapprehension that has existed in respect to this inquiry. Although statistics do not constitute the only proof of the great ultimate mortality from chloroform, they are assuredly the most convincing ; but as there are some persons so unacquainted with the principles of statistical investigation as not to place any confidence in its results, it is proper to state that the question of the propriety of using chloroform in operations by no means depends upon this proposition of an *ulterior* mortality. Had they been all reported or made generally known, it would have been universally acknowledged that the deaths forming the other two classes mentioned above, or those occurring at an earlier period, would alone constitute an amount of mortality which it is perfectly unjustifiable to produce for the prevention of the transient pain of ordinary operations.

" Are we, then, again to have our operating theatres filled with shrieks, and the unpractised surgeon unnerved by the sufferings of his patient?" By this question, it has by some, been strangely supposed that a satisfactory refutation is given to every objection against the use of chloroform; and there is implied in it a charge of cruelty against those to whom it is directed, as if cruelty is not more manifest in recklessness about a patient's life than about his ease. Fortunately, however, if their dangerous nature obliges us to abandon the use of intoxicating vapours in the great majority of operations, we should not, in our humane endeavours to prevent pain, be left without a resource. Insensibility can in most instances (and in almost all to a great and very useful extent) be perfectly produced, and with complete safety, by applications made to the part itself which is to be operated upon, and without the suspension of the patient's consciousness.

It is a singular circumstance, that both the general and local modes of preventing pain in operations should long have been familiarly known as capable of producing insensibility, and both avoided, on account, probably, of their supposed danger. I have already spoken of the mephitic vapour of the Grotto del Cane. Still better known was the benumbing effect of intense cold on parts exposed to it. But while the fears of the inhalation of vapours have unhappily been verified, those respecting cold have been proved to be groundless. For several years the local application of intense cold has been employed in surgical operations, not only without a single untoward occurrence, but with the immense additional advantage over chloroform of warding off that excess of inflammation from operation wounds which so often prevents their healing. It had not occurred previously to my investigation of the subject, that although long continued congelation, such as accidentally occurs in very cold climates, will injure the more isolated parts of the body, it may, when short and regulated, be a very different process; a process perfectly free from danger, yet so powerful, as not only to produce insensibility in operations, but to constitute a prompt and unfailing remedy in many inflammatory and painful diseases.*

---

* A minute is a sufficient period for congelation in operations, though a longer application may sometimes be desirable to secure its antiphlogistic as well as its anæsthetic powers. Some time ago, with a view to destroy painlessly

The only reason which can be assigned for the fact that cold has not yet generally superseded chloroform in many operations is, that its proper application requires a little more skill and involves a little more trouble. Nothing can be easier than to pour chloroform on a handkerchief and hold it under the patient's nose; but it requires some practice to congeal a part properly, and some pains to prepare the frigorific materials suitable for the degree of cold required. Yet surely these reasons would have formed no barrier to its adoption had surgeons been aware of the true character of the proceeding for which cold was proposed as a substitute. A conscientious practitioner thinks not of trouble when the life of his patient is at stake, and he is anxious to learn to do that perfectly which may be of service to him.*

---

the outer part of an occult cancerous tumour in the breast, I kept up congelation for nearly an hour, without causing the least permanent injury of the skin.

I am glad to mention this decisive fact, as it utterly demolishes the prejudice which still tends to delay that extensive use of the remedial agency of intense cold which is required to supply a great desideratum in therapeutics; for though cold has been used and much esteemed since the origin of medicine, its most efficient *dose* was unknown. Yet the medical journals furnish evidence that new and valuable applications of it are every now and then occurring. Even in deep seated disease of the viscera, it has been found an effectual resource when other remedies have failed. In the *Liverpool Medical Journal* for this month, there is a report of the use of congelation as a means of immediately and permanently suppressing phthisical vomiting; and, in a recent French medical journal, several cases of obstinate obstruction of the bowels are related, which were cured at the Hôtel Dieu by cold, after other means had been used in vain. It is true that the degree of cold in the latter instance was not so intense as that produced by frigorific mixtures; but, as the reporter justly states, the now well established innocuousness of this greater degree has emboldened physicians to employ ice with a degree of freedom which formerly would have been avoided. Under different circumstances, however, as when the part does not possess much vitality, a prolonged remedial congelation will destroy it, and may be usefully employed for such a purpose. In an interesting history of the various remedies adopted of late years in cancer, contained in the *Medical Times and Gazette* of this week, there is an account of the speedy removal by congelation of " a large flabby convex growth"; and M. Velpeau, in his *Treatise on Cancer*, speaks of its advantages in similar cases.

* Exaggerated notions, however, of this "trouble" are entertained. At a

It has not proceeded from want of sufficient evidence of its excellence that local insensibility from cold has not as yet been generally adopted. There are a great many reports of its successful use in the medical journals of Europe and America, and in works written by the respective operators. It has been employed in the excision of tumours by M. Velpeau, Mr. Paget, Mr. Bellingham, Mr. Erichsen, Mr. Ward, Mr. A. Johnson, Mr. Fleming, and others. Various surgeons have reported their successful use of it in the operation for hernia, in tracheotomy, amputation of the fingers, evulsion of the nails, breaking down nævi, opening abscesses, carbuncles, and whitlows, the extraction of foreign bodies, the removal of cicatrix, and operations on the eye. Half-a-dozen treatises by English and foreign dentists have described the use of congelation in operations on the teeth. Mr. Lawrence and M. Nelaton have prevented the pain of the actual cautery by it; and Mr. Langston Parker, the pain from caustics employed for the enucleation of cancer. One of the last reports referring to congelation which I have seen, mentions another employment of it in this disease by Mr. Stanley at St. Bartholomew's Hospital, namely, for the painless removal of the skin covering two scirrhous tumours previously to the application of chloride of zinc.*

In reference to the use of congelation in cancer, I may mention that this is by no means confined to these combinations of it with caustic; but it would be foreign to the pur-

---

recent inquest on a death from chloroform at St. Thomas's Hospital, it was stated that there was a difficulty experienced in placing the patient, who was about to have his finger amputated, under its influence. Would it not have been less troublesome to have dipped the finger for a few seconds into a glass of dissolving ice and salt, as was done with perfect success in a similar amputation, related at a late meeting of the Harveian Society? In estimating the comparative trouble of the two methods, we must not forget the various instrumental means of averting sudden death, with which every conscientious practitioner must be provided before administering chloroform; nor the hours spent in attempts at resuscitation by artificial respiration, galvanism, suspending the body by the feet, etc.

* A highly refrigerated mineral acid might, by means of an open cup or flat ring fitted to and pressed upon the part, be employed for the purpose of simultaneously benumbing and destroying.

pose of this paper to enter upon the consideration of the curative properties of intense cold, unless so far as they illustrate its utility in operations.

I shall only now remark in reference to its antiphlogistic properties, which are of the highest importance in this respect, that the fact of an adequate degree and continuance of cold so altering the functions of the vessels and nerves of the part subjected to it, as not only to arrest inflammation instantly, but to render the part incapable of this morbid affection some time afterwards, constitutes, from the extensive applicability of the remedial principle, one of the most important medical truths which have yet come to light.

The only defect in congelation, as a mode of producing insensibility in operations, is the small extent which its influence can penetrate from the surface. But in the greatest number of cases this objection does not hold. Even in amputation of limbs, the principal portion of the pain may be thus avoided, for that is produced by the incision of the skin and its dissection from the underlying flesh; and the separation of the skin from the surface of large tumours is, also, the most painful part of their excision. Congelation, however, might be conjoined with pressure, and either so long continued or produced by such powerful frigorific mixtures, as to remove this objection; or the mixture may be applied after the first incision, as has been practised with excellent effect in America. The mode of applying this agent is probably yet far from perfection, but the principles to be attended to in the procedure, are, I think, fully pointed out in my writings on the subject.*

---

* I have minutely described the mode of applying intense cold in operations in several papers in the *Medical Times and Gazette*, Nov. 11th, 1854; Nov. 24th, 1855; Feb. 14th, 1857; and, incidentally, in Treatises on its curative agency in Headache, Neuralgia, Rheumatism, and Cancer.

It were needless to notice another objection to congelation, that it is itself a cause of pain, as this has long since been declared groundless, but the following ludicrous artifice of an opponent deserves a remark in passing. In a popular article on Chloroform, by Dr. Simpson, in the *Encyclopedia Britannica*, congelation is called "frost-biting." As no one is better aware than

I think it would be difficult to bring forward a question connected with medicine on which the investigation and authority of an "Academy" is more required than that which I have now briefly and imperfectly stated; and which, it appears to me, cannot be otherwise speedily determined. A single death produced by a practice for which there is a complete and safe substitute is a lamentable and discreditable occurrence, for such a practice is condemned alike by the moral and statute law; but if great numbers are cut off by the use of intoxicating vapours for the avoidance of transient pain, even though this could not be otherwise prevented, the fact demands immediate notice and correction. The evidence which has been adduced proves that many die from the immediate effects of chloroform; others, within a few hours of its administration; and a very large number at more advanced periods, notwithstanding that the object for which it is administered might, in most instances, be fully attained without the slightest hazard. Yet, as respects the last class of deaths, or those caused by the ulterior agency of chloroform, it is proper to mention, that this disastrous error can hardly be said to reflect discredit on any one; for it was only discoverable by statistical investigation, and this, necessarily, could not be instituted until after a considerable lapse of time.

London, July 12th, 1857.

Dr. Simpson (who has often employed congelation remedially) that there is no resemblance between its effects and those of what is usually termed frost-bite, his knowledge of the power of names to excite prejudice, is as clearly shewn here, as when the significant phrase "excessive inebriation," originally used in America to express the effect of ether and chloroform, was so adroitly changed by him into the unsuggestive term, "anæsthesia."